To my mother, with love

First published in 2017 by Child's Play (International) Ltd
Ashworth Road, Bridgemead, Swindon SN5 7YD, UK

Published in USA in 2018 by Child's Play Inc
250 Minot Avenue, Auburn, Maine 04210

Distributed in Australia by Child's Play Australia Pty Ltd
Unit 10/20 Narabang Way, Belrose, Sydney, NSW 2085

ISBN 978-1-84643-931-5
L120517CPL07179315

Printed in Heshan, China

1 3 5 7 9 10 8 6 4 2

A catalogue record of this book
is available from the British Library

www.childs-play.com

Beyond the Fence

Maria Gulemetova

Thomas talked a lot. And Piggy had to listen.

Thomas knew what suited Piggy.

He always knew what they should play.

He just knew.

One day, Thomas' cousin came to visit.

Piggy took a walk.

"Nice to meet you," said Wild Pig.
"Why have you wrapped yourself up?"

"Do you mean these?" said Piggy.
"They're called clothes."

"Don't they get tangled when
you run through the bushes?"

"No. I never run."

"Oh, but running's fun. You should try it.
We can run together."

"I'd love to, but I have to go home now.
Please will you come again?"

"I will."

Piggy kept going to the place where he had met Wild Pig.

But he was never there.

Then one evening...

"I'm sorry I didn't come sooner," said Wild Pig.
"I fell in a trap and it took a few days to get out.
Shall we run in the forest?"

"I'd love to, but I'm not allowed to go beyond the fence."

"Really? Well then, I'll come back for another chat.
Tomorrow at sunset."

"That would be lovely."

The next morning, Thomas' cousin left.

At sunset, Piggy had to listen to a story.

Maybe Wild Pig would come again tomorrow.

The next day at sunset...

"Please excuse me for a moment."

"Where IS that silly pig?"

But Piggy was already beyond the fence.

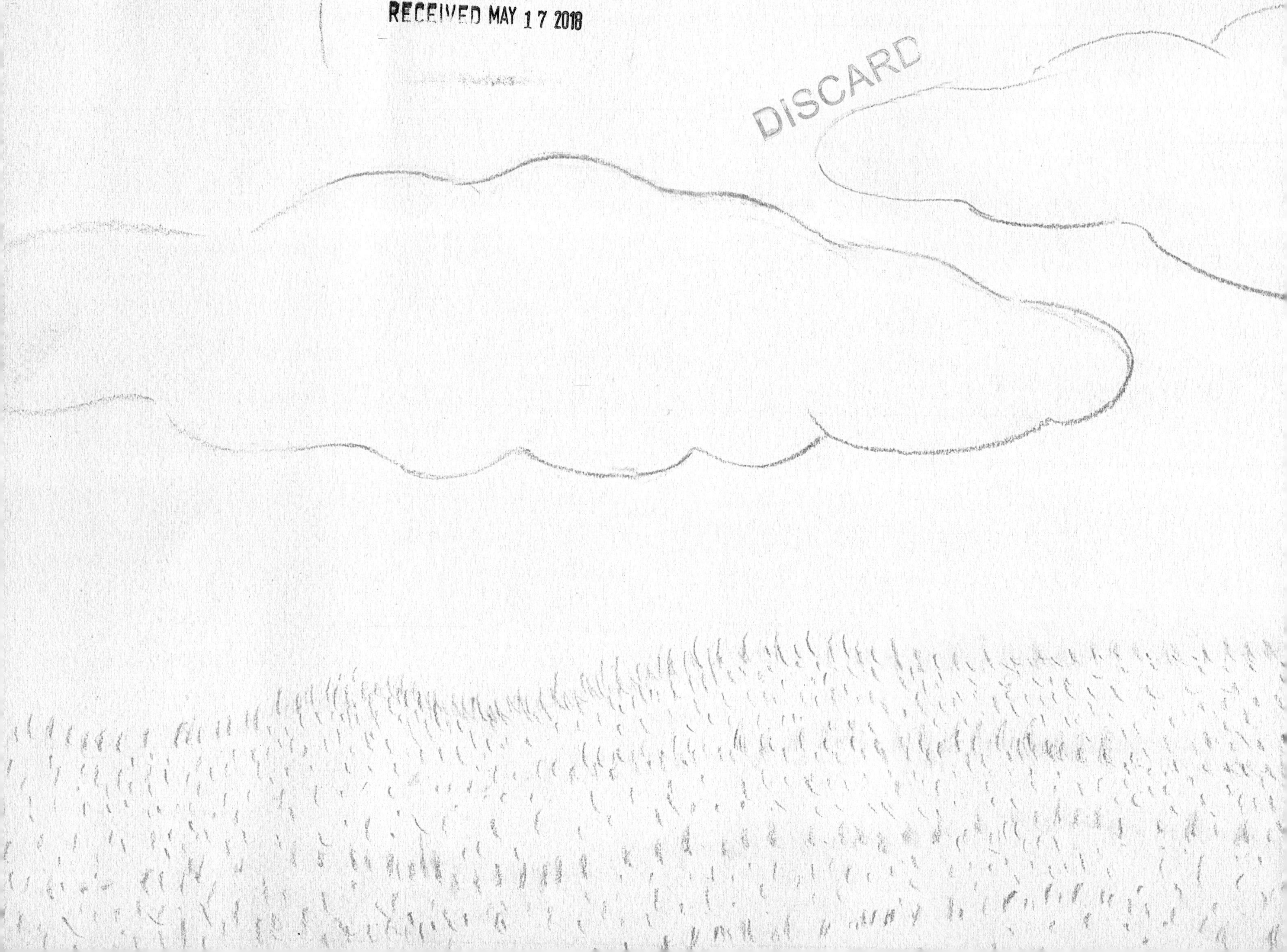